BV

KT-239-186

70002185813X

Text copyright © 2000 Sam Godwin
Illustrations copyright © 2000 Tony Morris

Series concept: Wendy Knowles

Published in Great Britain in 2000
by Hodder Wayland, an imprint of
Hodder Children's Books

A Catalogue record for this book is available from
the British Library.

ISBN 0 7500 2905 6

Printed in Hong Kong by Wing King Tong Co. Ltd.

Hodder Children's Books
A division of Hodder Headline plc
338 Euston Road, London NW1 3BH

Sister on the Street

The story of Mother Teresa

Sam Godwin

WORCESTERSHIRE COUNTY COUNCIL	
813	
Cypher	14.02.02
	£4.50

Illustrated by Tony Morris

HODDER
Wayland

an imprint of Hodder Children's Books

Mother Teresa

Mother Teresa was born Agnes Gonxha
Bejaxhiu to Catholic Albanian parents in 1910.
She grew up in Skopje, a town in Serbia (now
called Macedonia) in Eastern Europe. Agnes was
a religious child, spending a lot of time in prayer.
At the age of 18, she travelled to Ireland and
joined the orders of the Sisters of Loreto as a
novice nun. It was then that she took the name
of Teresa. Before long, she went to India to
continue her studies and to do missionary work.
After taking her final vows, she became the
principal of a Catholic school for wealthy girls
in Calcutta. But the poverty that Mother Teresa
saw outside the convent in Calcutta, led her to
set up her own order, The Missionaries of Charity.

As her work spread to the far corners of the
world, Mother Teresa became a spokesperson
for the poor, sick and unfairly treated. She was
awarded the Nobel Peace Prize in 1979 and died
in 1997. Even after her death, the work of the
Missionaries of Charity continues to help the
poor of the world.

Chapter 1

It was nearly going-home time and I felt
tired and hungry. Geography was my
favourite lesson and Mother Teresa my
favourite teacher, but today was too hot
for lessons and I was desperate to get
home so I could have some cold mango
juice. The end of lesson bell rang,
interrupting Mother Teresa in
mid-sentence, and everyone started
putting their books in their satchels. I
placed my atlas under my arm, where
everyone could admire it. It was brand
new, with colourful maps and pictures.

As I was walking to the door, Mother Teresa stopped me. 'Could you help me with the map, Sunita?' she asked.

Mother Teresa had pinned a huge world map to the blackboard for the lesson and she needed help with putting it away.

'I heard your sister Aisha is back in Calcutta,' she said as we folded the map.

'She got back yesterday,' I said. 'I'm sure she'll come and see you soon.'

'I'd love to see her,' Mother Teresa smiled. 'She was a very good pupil and a credit to St. Mary Entally School, just as you are, Sunita.'

I blushed. It's nice to be praised by a teacher, especially one who also happens to be the school principal, but I was glad that all the other girls had gone out of the classroom.

Mother Teresa placed the folded map in a drawer. Then she started arranging the books neatly on her desk. 'Is your sister still working at the lawyer's?' she asked.

'Yes,' I said. 'But she is giving her work up soon, to get married. She's going to live in Delhi with her husband's family.'

Mother Teresa smiled. 'It must be nice to have a home of your own, and children. But we are not all called to the same vocation.' She finished tidying up the books and sighed. 'Have you given any thought to your future, Sunita?'

'I want to travel,' I said. 'Like you, Mother. I want to go from one country to another, seeing all there is to see. I want to visit Ireland to see your Mother House, and England to see Buckingham Palace. And perhaps I'll go to Egypt too, to visit the pyramids you told us about.'

'Travel broadens the mind,' agreed Mother Teresa kindly. Perhaps she was thinking of her own travels around the world, from her own home in Serbia to Ireland, and then to India on a boat. Mother Teresa had often told us about her journey to India, how sick she had been on the boat and how miserable because there was no Catholic priest to say Mass.

I had no intention of suffering during my travels. I wanted to ride in the first-class coaches of trains, in the best cabins on fantastic cruise liners. I wanted to eat the most delicious food and wear the most fabulous gowns from Paris. I dreamt of being rich.

Mother Teresa looked out of the window, past the neat lawns and playgrounds of our school. Beyond the walls, lay the slums of Calcutta, where the poorest people lived. Only a few girls from there had ever come to our school, and only two had stayed for more than a term. 'We go where God asks us to go,' Mother Teresa said. 'Some of us to enchanted places faraway, some of us to undiscovered worlds closer to home. There are wonderful things to experience everywhere, even in the bustees.'

Her words puzzled me. The bustees outside the school walls were not a place anyone in their right mind would want to visit. What wonderful things could you possibly find there? Sometimes I didn't understand Mother Teresa at all.

Chapter 2

'Are you going to see Mother Teresa?' I asked my sister Aisha as we sat in our living room, drinking tea.

'Why would she bother to go and see that nun for?' scoffed my brother Sunil. 'She's not a pupil at St. Mary's anymore.'

'Mother Teresa would like to see her,' I argued. 'She likes to keep in touch with her old pupils.'

'Nuns don't care about their pupils,' Sunil said. 'They only care about their convent and their religion. They're European, after all. When did white people ever do anything for us? They're only here to grab what they can.'

I flared up, 'Mother Teresa isn't like that. She genuinely cares about people, any people, including Indians. Sometimes she goes unnoticed into the slums and helps the poor and the sick. She comforts them and gives them medicine. That's more than you will ever do for your own people.'

I thought that my brother would be impressed with Mother Teresa's work, but he wasn't. 'If she likes Indians so much, why does she keeping on wearing European clothes in this hot weather? Why doesn't she wear a sari?'

'Because she is a nun,' I shouted, losing my patience, 'and nuns have to wear habits, like soldiers have to wear uniforms.'

Sunil grinned. Like most brothers, he enjoyed upsetting his younger sister. 'No,' he said. 'Your precious Mother Teresa wears a habit because she thinks she is superior to us all.'

Aisha put down her tea. 'Sunil has a point,' she said. 'It's better not to get too close to Europeans, no matter how caring they seem to be. In the end they always go back home and leave the poor of India to suffer on their own.'

'Mother Teresa would never leave India,' I said stubbornly. 'She's different.'

Chapter 3

But was she different? The Friday
following my argument with Sunil, I met
my friend Shamila in the playground.
'Have you heard the news?' she gasped.
'Mother Teresa is leaving St. Mary's.'

I looked at her in shock. Mother Teresa
had been principal at our school ever since
anyone could remember. No one could
imagine St. Mary's without her.

'Where is she going?' I asked.

Shamila shrugged. 'No one knows for sure. Some say she is going to the convent in Darjeeling. Others say she is going back to Ireland. Bimla from the third year thinks she's leaving the Order to marry an English doctor.'

'Never,' I said. 'Mother Teresa is far too old to get married. She's thirty-eight years old.'

But many of the other girls had heard the rumour too. Some asked the teachers and other sisters if they knew what was going on, but it was all news to them too. I decided to ask Mother Teresa myself, just so I could tell everyone the truth, so I offered to take the attendance register to her office.

'Mother's not in for the day,' said another sister, taking the register from my hands. 'She's visiting some sisters on Lower Circular Road. She won't be back till late.'

As I walked back to my classroom, my head was filled with doubt and Aisha's words echoed in my mind... 'It's best not to get too close to Europeans. In the end they all go back home and leave the poor of India to suffer on their own.'

Was Mother Teresa really going to desert us after all? Was she going back home to Europe? I was soon to find out.

Chapter 4

It was late on Sunday afternoon. Shamila and I had been helping out at the boarding school, which shares the same grounds as St. Mary's. The younger children there were putting on a play for the end of term and we had volunteered to help make costumes and paint scenery. As we were walking towards the main gate, Shamila noticed a light in the convent chapel.

'What's going on in there, I wonder?' she asked. 'The chapel is not normally open at this time of the day, not even on a Sunday.'

'I have no idea,' I said, 'and we're not finding out. The chapel is out of bounds for us.'

That was the wrong thing to say to Shamila. She's easily the most curious person on earth. She started walking across the lawn and I followed her, so I wouldn't be left alone.

There was someone in the chapel. We peeped in and saw Mother Teresa standing

in the sacristy with Mother Du Cenacle, the former school principal and her superior. There was a priest too, one we had often seen at school but had never talked to. He spoke in a different accent from Mother Teresa's or Mother Du Cenacle's. To our astonishment, Mother Du Cenacle was crying into her handkerchief.

'Here they are, father,' said Mother Teresa. She picked up three white saris with blue borders and placed them on a table. The priest blessed them.

'That's curious,' said Shamila who saw mystery and intrigue in everything. 'Who are the saris for? Do you think Mother Teresa is going to turn Indian and marry a Bengali doctor?'

'Don't be silly,' I said, 'maybe they're a gift for someone. They're only cotton saris.'

The priest finished the blessing and Mother Teresa folded the saris away in a cardboard box. 'Thank you, father,' she said. 'Now I must go and prepare some lessons. We have so much to do this term.'

'Did you hear that?' I said to Shamila as we hurried back across the lawn to the school gates, 'Mother Teresa is preparing lessons for next term. She can't be leaving after all.'

Chapter 5

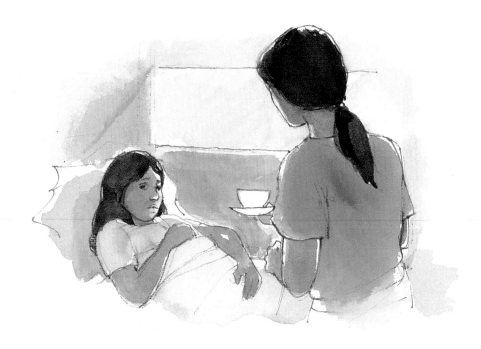

On Monday morning I woke up with a cold. Ma told me to stay in bed and Prya, our servant, made me lots of hot, herbal tea. By Wednesday my cold had developed into full-blown flu. I was bedridden for days. Shamila came to see me every day, mostly to fill me in on local gossip.

Then, one afternoon, she stumbled into my room, wide-eyed with excitement. 'You've missed the biggest event of the century,' she said. 'Mother Teresa HAS left St. Mary's after all. She's gone to Patna, to study nursing.'

Patna? Nursing? I couldn't believe my ears. 'Are you sure?' I said.

Shamila sat on the edge of my bed. 'Of course, I'm sure. There was a presentation at the boarding school and a farewell concert with Bengali songs. Everyone was crying their eyes out.' She stood up again, 'Perhaps she is going to marry an English doctor after all.'

'Don't be ridiculous,' I said. 'Mother Teresa is too dedicated to give up her work; she must have some other plan.'

Just then Sunil came into the room, looking like the cat that had got the cream. 'Heard the news?' he said. 'Your precious nun has gone and dumped you. I bet she'll go back to Europe, to live in some fancy convent where they get good food and nice cool weather.'

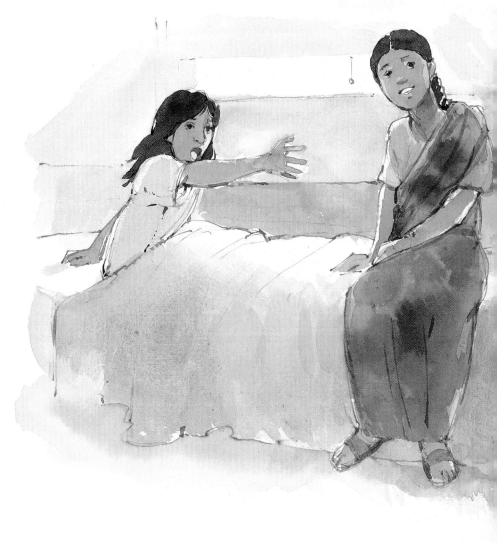

Sunil didn't finish the sentence because
I threw a pillow at him. He ducked but it
hit him.

'Why do you defend the old nun?' he
said. 'What is she to you?'

'I don't know,' I said. And it was true, I had no idea why I felt such a connection with a school principal, especially one that had let me down and was leaving us.

Chapter 6

It was a hot Sunday in December. Shamila and I were sitting on the verandah drinking tea and chatting. Prya, our maid, interrupted us. 'You wouldn't happen to have a spare workbook for my Ravi, would you, Miss Sunita?' she asked.

'I think I do,' I said.

Shamila looked up from her teacup. 'I didn't know your Ravi went to school, Prya,' she said.

'Oh yes,' replied Prya proudly. 'My Ravi goes to the new school in Motijhil.'

Shamila and I looked at each other. Motijhil was the terrible slum outside our school. There were hardly any decent buildings for people to live in there, let alone a school. The people lived out on the streets, wrapped in ragged blankets. What was Prya talking about?

'It's not much of a school, yet,' she continued. 'We have no building with classrooms, just a big tree for the children to sit under. We're going to buy slates and a blackboard soon, so the teacher won't have to write the lessons on the ground with a stick. But my Ravi's learning the alphabet already. He has milk every day and he's learnt a lot about cleanliness too. Yesterday he won a bar of soap for getting his sums right. Now the principal says she might get a hut for five rupees. I said to her, I said, 'Mother Teresa I'll..."

'Hold on a second,' I said.
'Did you say 'Mother Teresa?'.

'Oh yes,' said Prya, her eyes shining with pride. 'I think she used to be principal at your school, but she's my Ravi's principal now. She went to Patna for a few months, to learn how to care for the sick and the dying. But she's back in Calcutta now, teaching again.'

I looked at Shamila in triumph. So my beloved Mother Teresa hadn't deserted India after all. She hadn't gone back to Europe like Sunil had insisted. On the contrary, she'd given up her cushy life at our school, to work just around the corner, looking after the really needy. Because Mother Teresa cared. I stood up and turned to Prya.

'Tell Ravi he can have all my spare copybooks,' I said, 'and all my pencils and rubbers too. And there's something else I want to give your school principal. But I want to give it to her in person.'

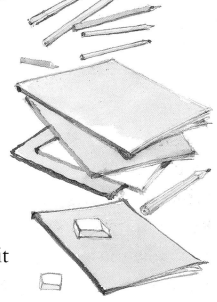

Chapter 7

Shamila and I ventured into Motijhil, followed by five of our classmates. Although we'd been to Entally every day, we'd never ventured into the bustee. Of course, we saw poor people all the time, huddled on the side of the streets, begging for a rupee or two. But we'd never seen the poverty we saw that day in Motijhil.

The huts were small and crowded. There was a terrible smell in the air, which came from the open sewers that ran into the tank they called 'the lake'. There were naked, dirty children everywhere, some of whom had a leg or an arm missing.

Then we saw Mother Teresa, our former principal who had lived in an immaculate convent surrounded by neatly cut lawns, teaching ragged children under a tree. At first we didn't recognise her. She wasn't wearing a nun's habit but a sari – one of the saris Shamila and I had seen the priest blessing in the chapel. Most of my friends gasped. They'd never seen a European woman in a sari before, only Indians. And what's more, Mother Teresa was wearing sandals. She was practically barefoot. That shocked us too, for Europeans never showed their toes, not even in the hottest of summers. For the first time in her life, Shamila was speechless.

Mother Teresa looked up from her pupils and saw us. She smiled the old, comfortable smile I knew so well. 'Sunita,' she said. 'Welcome to our school.'

I ran forward, leaving the others behind. 'I've brought you something,' I said, 'for your lessons.'

'What is it?' asked Mother Teresa.

'My atlas,' I said. 'You're going to need an atlas for your geography lessons.'

'But *you* need the atlas,' said Mother Teresa. 'You're going to Ireland and England and Egypt, remember?'

'Oh no, I don't need an atlas any more,' I said, for I had suddenly realised why I felt such a connection with my old school principal. I too wanted to help change the world, to make the slums a better place for people to live in. My future had nothing to do with luxury trains and cruise liners. I wanted to spend my life helping to sort out the unfairness in the world. I could learn to teach, nurse, bring hope into people's lives. Like Mother Teresa, I wanted to be a sister on the street.

45

Glossary

bustees an Indian word for slums in which very
poor people live

habit a cloak-like garment worn, mostly in the
past, by religious people, especially nuns
and monks.

Mother House the head house of a religious
order

missionary a person who travels to another
country to do good work, usually of a
religious nature.

novice a new member of a religious order,
before they have taken their final vows.

order a group of people, usually religious, who
have the same leader and are united by
their beliefs and vows.

rupee the unit of money used in India

sacristy a special part of a church where the
priests dress for ceremonies. Sacred objects
used for worship are also kept there.

sari a long, cotton or silk dress traditionally
worn by Indian women.

vocation a call, usually considered to be from
God, to spend one's life helping others
through action and prayer.